W9-BTM-390

GEAUGA WEST LIBRARY

To Yumi, with many thanks for a wonderful
day at Polka Dot Penguin Pottery—L.L.

For all the moms and dads, grandmas and grandpas, and children
who bring their creativity to Polka Dot Penguin Pottery—Y.H.

Text copyright © 2011 by Lenore Look • Jacket art and interior illustrations copyright © 2011 by Yumi Heo • All rights reserved. Published in the United States by Schwartz & Wade Books, an imprint of Random House Children's Books, a division of Random House, Inc., New York. Schwartz & Wade Books and the colophon are trademarks of Random House, Inc. • Visit us on the Web! www.randomhouse.com/kids • Educators and librarians, for a variety of teaching tools, visit us at www.randomhouse.com/teachers

Library of Congress Cataloging-in-Publication Data
Look, Lenore. • Polka Dot Penguin Pottery / by Lenore Look ; illustrated by Yumi Heo.—1st ed. • p. cm. • Summary: A visit to a pottery shop and the encouragement of family and friends not only provide Aspen the opportunity to paint something beautiful, they also help her get past her writer's block. ISBN 978-0-375-86332-5 (trade) — ISBN 978-0-375-96332-2 (glb) • [1. Creative ability—Fiction. 2. Authorship—Fiction. 3. Pottery craft—Fiction. 4. Chinese Americans—Fiction.] I. Heo, Yumi, ill. II. Title. • PZ7.L8682Pol 2011 • [E]—dc22 • 2009047161

The text of this book is set in Kennerley. • The illustrations were rendered in oil, pencil, and collage. • Book design by Rachael Cole

MANUFACTURED
IN MALAYSIA
10 9 8 7 6 5 4 3 2 1
First Edition

Random
House Children's
Books supports the
First Amendment
and celebrates the
right to read.

Polka Dot Penguin Pottery

by lenore look   illustrated by yumi heo

schwartz & wade books · new york

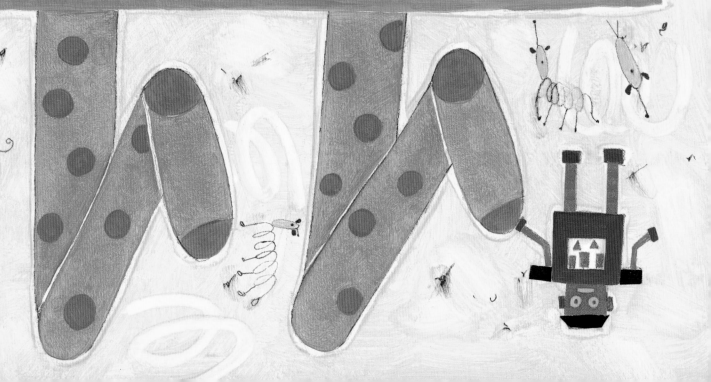

My name is Aspen Colorado Kim Chee Lee. Actually, that's my nom de plume—my writing name, not my real name. I'm an author. I write stories about monkeys and elephants, aliens and robots, and, sometimes, about me.

Once upon a time an elephant named Ella Rose and a monkey named Matteo went to China together to see the Great Wall when they got there, they couldn't find the wall because aliens and robots kidnapped it.

I work in my tree house, where there's a sign that says, "Writer at work, do not disturb," and when you flip it over, it says, "Writer at play, come up and stay."

writer at work
do not disturb

This is how to write.

First button on
your writing jacket.

Then stuff your
pockets with
seaweed crackers.

Then sit very still
and think.

Last but not least, choose words
and line them up—like a fruit seller
who chooses her best mangoes and
pomegranates and bananas and
puts them on display. And when
you're done—yay!—a story.

But lately, writing hasn't been much fun. In fact,
you can't even call it writing at all! All my pages
are blank, blank, blank. My gunggung and pohpoh
call it Writer's Block.

"Don't worry," says PohPoh. "Your characters
are just on vacation. They'll be back."

"Maybe you need to take a break and just
hang out," suggests GungGung.

Charise's Cookie Caper

Book It Here

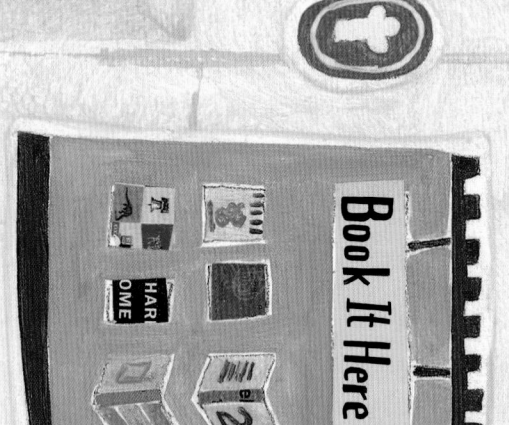

Pet Palace

So off we go, down into town past the cookie shop, the bookstore, and Pet Palace, with the water dishes for dogs and squirrels out front. I follow GungGung, PohPoh, and baby Olivia through the morning chill, the wind licking my nose and whistling in my ears.

Finally, GungGung opens the door to a place I've walked past a million times—Polka Dot Penguin Pottery—but have never gone into.

Inside, it feels like summer. A lady who is sweeping stops and smiles like a flower facing the sun. "Welcome!" she says. "My name is Yumi. What would you like to paint?" She ties an apron on me.

Paint? Me? Suddenly, I'm so excited, I can't answer. My words are swirling around the shop and I cannot catch them.

Instead, I rush over to the shelves of One Thousand
Things to Paint and look them over in three seconds flat.
I pick an Easter egg, just like that.

The door jingles open. Twin boys come in with their mom. Yumi greets them by name, Lefty and Righty. They must be regulars. They rush over to the shelves and grab a robot and a fire engine.

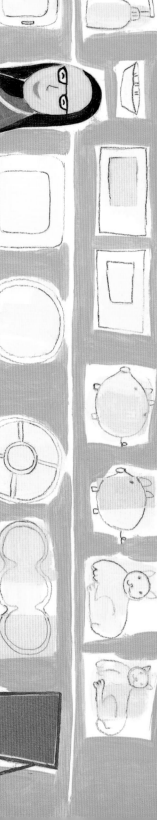

I sit down next to PohPoh and Olivia, who is too little to paint anything properly. She just makes a mess. I turn my egg over and over; it is blank, like a piece of paper.

"Hey," Lefty and Righty say, bumping the table and spilling my paint tray a little as they sit down across from me.

"Careful," their mom warns them.

"Sorry."

"Your first time here?" their mom asks me.

I nod.

"We'll show you how it's done," says Righty.

"Yeah," says Lefty, "just do like me."

In no time their robot and fire engine look amazing!

But my egg is still blank.

The door jingles again and the wind blows in my friend Ivy, her brother Luther, and their mom. Ivy picks a heart box and Luther picks a dinosaur.

They sit, and for a moment, neither of them moves. Then, out of their paint bottles, they squeeze flowers and grass, hearts and sparkly dinosaur skin.

"How did you do that?" I ask, peering into a paint bottle named Sailboat White.

"Easy," says Ivy, painting her name on her heart box. "But you have to stay super-still."

"And wait for something to happen," Luther chirps.

Sounds like writing to me. But it's super-hard to sit super-still. My feet are tapping. My legs are jiggling. The tag on my dress is scratching.

I wait.

Nothing happens.

It's starting to feel like a party in here! A dinosaur pirouettes. A mermaid sings. Martta, who is Yumi's helper, is balancing a hundred shiny, breakable things, hot from the kiln, and trying hard *not* to dance. And Olivia is wiggling to the music and drooling.

Yumi is working super-fast. She swipes a credit card. She answers the phone. She brings sponges and a bucket of water to our table, for "just in case." She greets a birthday party that comes in with balloons and presents. Everything is happening all at once!

Still, nothing is happening with me. I am holding my brush in the air—stiff, frozen, and useless, like an ice cream stick without the ice cream.

I think I have Pottery Block.

My head clunks on the table like a bowling ball and everything looks like it's underwater. I breathe in. I breathe out. I don't breathe at all. I reach—dip my brush in paint— and touch it to my egg.

And as soon as I do, something happens. The paint drips.

"Oh no!" I cry. "It's ruined!" I put my head down on the table. My arms hang low. I close my eyes.

"Do you need some water?" GungGung asks.

PohPoh rubs my back. "Maybe it'll help if we paint something together?" she says. I hear their footsteps going toward the shelves of One Thousand Things to Paint.

I look at my egg.
It's a mess, all right.
I touch my brush to it.
I look at it again.
It's still a mess.

So I make it messier,
and the color spreads.
   I see a tree in the
mess and make some
branches.

Then I add
some pink and
purple leaves.
Not bad.
I paint a green
sky with big red
flowers floating
like clouds.

Wow! This
feels like writing
too—when you put
down one word,
and—surprise!—
more words follow.

Soon green
butterflies are
fluttering in the
orange grass.

Around me, heads turn.

Eyes stare.

Polka Dot Penguin Pottery stops.

"I need just a few dabs," I say, "for my dress."

Then it's done.

This is my egg.

These are the jaws that dropped.

And when I get home, I run straight to
my tree house, where I flip the sign to say,
"Writer at work, do not disturb."
And this is the story that began with
just hanging out.

Painting Pottery is fun and easy

1. Choose your pottery.

2. Clean off your pottery

3. — Soak your sponge in water squeeze out your sponge. Wipe off your pottery all over.

3. Paint your pottery.

— Light colors first and darker color on top.

— wash out your brush and dry it on your sponge when changing colors.

TURKEY TAFFY